Reading Comprehension Passages:

Congolese Tales

Christophe Kambaji

TANZANIA EDUCATIONAL PUBLISHERS LTD

Tanzania Educational Publishers Ltd,
TEPU House,
Uganda road, Plot No. 45 Block MDA,
Mob: +255 685 997583/ +255 758 147871
Email: tepultd@yahoo.com
Website: www.tepu.co.tz
P.O. Box 1222,
Bukoba, Tanzania.

ISBN 978 9987 07 079 4

Contents

Introduction

This book is a collection of eleven tales from the Democratic Republic of Congo. They belong to the oral tradition. They have been transmitted from mouth to mouth to younger generations. They hand down traditions and customs from one generation to the next one. The protagonists of the tales are human beings, animals and objects. The animals take on human characteristics: greediness, jealousy, honesty and empathy.

The tales are told to children by   adults in the evenings around a fire or under a blue and starry sky. They are not told aimlessly. Their objective is to inculcate in children's mind values which will enable them to have harmonious relations with the members of their communities, to be wise enough to cope successfully with life's challenges and situations. And so children are taught to take into consideration the recommendations and instructions of more experienced people, to be considerate to other people, to be humble, wise and cautious.

They are rendered aware that, in life, every human being must be responsible of his deeds and will reap what he has sown. The tales also help children develop astounding capacities for memorization. Some tales are punctuated with songs. The latter help children to have the sense of rhetoric and rhythm.

This book is intended for students of English at advanced level. At the end of each tale there is an English glossary the aim of which is to help students to have a better understanding of the tales and to enrich their vocabulary. It also contains exercises which are in connection with the tales and the exploitation of which runs as follows:

1. Comprehension questions

They consist of simple questions, multiple choice questions and true/false statements. Concerning multiple choice questions, there will be alternatives that should be screened off carefully by the students. The latter will have to support or to determine why a particular statement is true or false.

They will also have the task of changing false statements into correct ones. There are sequences that include closed answers.

2. The reordering of some sentences closely connected with the tales

Sentences expressing key ideas of the tales are presented in disorder. The learners should put them in the correct order so as to make up a chronological sequence. This sequence will help them make summaries of the tales.

About the way summaries should be made, here are some tips. Students should:

a-make a carefull selection of the main ideas;

b-connect these ideas by providing bridges from one idea to another. There should not be any sudden and unexpected transition betwen these ideas;

c-eliminate irrelevent and unnecessary ideas;

d-give the summary an air of simplicity;

e-write down the ideas in a coherent sequence and logical order.

3. Lexis

This part turns around collocation exercises, the matching of some words and phrases with their definitions or meanings, filling gaps with words from the tales and opposites quiz.

There are also exercises helping the learners to find out nouns stemming from some verbs.

4. Sentence completion

In this exercise the learners are asked to restate some parts of the tales in order to complete some sentences .This exercise has the advantage of testing both comprehension and expression.

5. Discussion points

As most of the tales bear some moral lessons, I have conceived some discussion points with a view to stirring up open class debates .These discussion points will give   the learners the opportunity of expressing more freely their opinions and ideas. And so they should not be passive readers; but they should react to what they read. These points are stimuli for fluency practice and are very open.

6. Creative writing skills

They consist of exercises in which imagination plays an important role. There are pre-reading tasks in which the learners are asked to do some grammar exercises (asking some questions) or to predict the contents of some tales.

For such exercises a word limit is always suggested. This task is twofold: to stimulate the learners' imagination and to promote their productive skills.

This book has two sections: Section 'A' is made up of the Comprehension Passages, Questions and Exercises. Section 'B' is made up of Answers to Some Questions and Exercises. The main purpose is to enable the student compare his/her answers with the ones provided. This means that he/she should first answer the Questions and do the Exercises and later make the comparison.

Christophe KAMBAJI
Avenue du Derby, 7/6
1050 Brussels
BELGIUM
Telephone: 322 733 0937
Email: christophekambaji@outlook.com

SECTION A

COMPREHENSION PASSAGES, QUESTIONS AND EXERCISE

CHAPTER

Bindu and the Calabash

Pre-reading task

Ask 5 questions about the three first paragraphs

A man called Bindu was living in a village with his wife and his children. A t that time there was plenty of food in the village. But, one day a famine broke out suddenly and the village suffered heavily from it. And as a consequence, Bindu's wife and children, emaciated and exhausted, were lying sprawled on the ground. On seeing this, Bindu decided to go into the forest to look for some food. As he was passing next to a bush, he heard a voice calling him. He turned around the bush and saw a calabash stuck to some thorns. The calabash mournfully said to him:

"These thorns are causing me harm. Please help me get out of them, and I'll reward you."
Bindu plunged his arms into the thorns and got the calabash out. The calabash thanked him and said:

"Now take me to your home and I'll be of a great assistance to you."

Bindu carried the calabash and went back to his village. When his wife and his children saw that he was coming back only with a calabash, they started sobbing. But the calabash calmed them down and said:

"I can be filled with whatever you want. Now ask me for what you want."

Bindu's woman replied: " We are terribly hungry. Please be filled with some rice." Immediately the calabash was filled with some rice. And the whole family could eat more than enough.

Then, Bindu forbade his wife to report this event to anyone. But Bindu's wife did not follow this instruction and reported it to her neighbour. And the latter let it know to her sister. And finally, this event came to the ears of the village chief. As the chief realized that the calabash could be filled with all sorts of riches, he ordered it to be taken to his court. On hearing this, Bindu became very dispirited.

Some days later, the famine broke out again in the village.Bindu went again into the forest, and passing next to a bush, he heard again a call. He stopped and saw a big, gleaming stone amidst the thorns.

Then he screamed and exclaimed: "What a beautiful stone!" Hardly had he uttered these words that a painful blow fell upon his head. "That will be of a great lesson to you," said the stone. " I am not a big stone, I am a big pebble. And I strike whoever dares calling me *stone* insisted the 'stone'."

Bindu took this stone, wrapped it in a loincloth and brought it to the village chief. When the village chief saw the stone, he sniggered and said: "You've brought me only that thing!"

Then, the stone jumped onto the village chief. The chief started screaming and cursing the stone. The stone crushed his nose and jumped onto his chin. On hearing the chief crying, all the members of his court rushed towards him. When they saw this jumping stone, they, in turn, began to cry and to say: "What a stone! It's jumping by its own."

The stone became more and more furious. It smashed into skulls and legs of some villagers.
It overturned some of them and struck some others. It caused a lot of damage across the village; and when the chief realized that he had fallen into a trap, he gave back Bindu his calabash and never claimed for it.

QUESTIONS AND EXERCISES

I: Choose the right answer by writing its letter in the box on the right.

1. Bindu was:
    a)   polyginous
    b)   monogamous
    c)   single

2. Bindu's family:
    a)   followed him into the forest
    b)   moved to another village
    c)   remained in the village

3. The calabash was filled with:
    a)   some jewellery
    b)   something to eat
    c)   some rice

4. Bindu's wife spoke about the calabash to:
    a)   the villagers
    b)   the village chief
    c)   someone living near her

5. The village chief ordered the calabash to:
   a)   be exhibited in the village
   b)   be dispatched to a neighbouring village
   c)   be given to him

6. When the village chief saw the stone, he:
   a)   showed respect
   b)   remained indifferent
   c)   laughed sarcastically

II: Match the words with their definitions

1. Famine	a. hard fruit ;its shell is used as a bowl
2. Forest	b. a large area covered with trees and bushes
3. Bush	c. a small roundish stone
4. Pebble	d. very tired
5. Calabash	e. extreme shortage of food
6. Skull	f. the bones of the head
7. Exhausted	g. uncleared wild area with a lot of small plant

III: Match the statements in table A with those in table B

A

1.   Bindu decided
2.   Bindu's wife and children
3.   Bindu told his wife
4.   The village chief started
5.   The big stone

B

a. could eat more than enough
b. not to report to anyone what had happened
c. to go into the forest
d. screaming and cursing the stone.
e. smashed into the skulls and legs of some villagers.

IV: Put the following sentences in the correct order
1. When the chief saw the stone, he laughed sarcastically.
2. Bindu heard a voice calling him from the bush.
3. Bindu got the calabash out of the stone.
4. A famine broke out and spread all over the village.
5. Bindu and his family were living in a village.
6. Bindu went into the village to look for some food.
7. Bindu brought the calabash to the village.
8. The calabash was filled with some rice.
9. The village chief ordered the calabash to be carried to the court.
10. Bindu went again into the forest.

V: Find phrases in the tale that mean
1. We are extremely suffering from hunger.
2. Bindu ordered his wife to let no one know what had happened.
3. Bindu took the calabash and returned to the village.
4. Bindu's wife did not heed her husband's recommendation.
5. Bindu put a piece of cloth around the stone

VI. Which statement corresponds best to this tale? Explain
1. Greediness can generate harmful consequences
2. Revealing confidential talks is not beneficial
3. Don't get your ears tickled by gossips
4. Keeping secrets can lead to an advantage
5. It is wise to reflect before acting
VI. Write a summary of this tale (100 words):

Glossary
Amidst: among.
Dispirited: discouraged, in low spirits.
Emaciated: extremely thin.

Exhausted: very tired.
Gleaming: shining.
Mournfully: weeping, shedding tears with grief and sorrow.
Pebble: small roundish stone.
Thorn: short hard pointed shrub of a plant.
To be filled with: to be full of.
To break out: to start suddenly, to happen suddenly.
To curse: to say, to utter words intended to wish bad luck to
          someone.
To fall into a trap: to be ensnared, to be cheated and caught out.
To scream: to cry loudly.
To smash into: to hit very hard.
To snigger: to mock disrespectfully.
To sob: to cry in a tumultuous way.
To utter: to say, to pronounce.

2

CHAPTER

A Haughty Girl

Pre-reading task

From the headline, predict the content of this tale (60 words). Use the following words and phrases in the box.

> bright complexion, defectless, pretty girl, young boy, to marry her, basket, market, flexible hair, soft eyes, good-looking

Khenge was a pretty girl. However, she had the habit of despising other people, of considering them as base as dogs and of saying nay to all those who had asked her to marry her. She used to say that she wanted to get married with a smart young boy endowed with a bright complexion and who, at the same time, had to be defectless.

One day, Khenge went to the market to sell her vegetables. After, she started walking across the market; she met a young boy at the bottom of the market. This boy had a dazzling beauty and smartness: he had a brown complexion, very dark and flexible hair, soft eyes and highly-sharpened fingers with clean nails. He was very good looking and had no physical imperfection. Khenge realized that he was the kind of boy she was looking for. The boy, in turn, after glancing at her, found she was very beautiful. Both of them stared at each other longingly. Then, the young boy greeted Khenge and asked for her name. Khenge mentioned it.

The boy told Khenge that he wanted to marry her. Khenge agreed immediately. That is why he asked her to go back home to get all her valuable items and to come back and join him at the market. Khenge ran back home, took her valuable items and her other belongings. She put them into a basket, came back to the market and joined the young boy. Then, they headed for the young boy's village. The boy had a flute and started singing as follows:

Upon hearing this song, Khenge was baffled. They walked for a long time. Suddenly, Khenge noticed that the coat that the young boy was wearing had disappeared. While they were going their way, Khenge noticed that, this time, the boy's tie had mysteriously vanished. Some kilometers farther, the boy threw his shirt and trousers away. Finally, all the boy's clothes went out of sight. The boy remained completely naked.

Khenge managed to control her emotions; she asked the boy what had occurred to his clothes. The boy answered that they did not belong to him; that he had borrowed them and that now he is giving them back to their owners. Khenge became frightened. Fear assailed her. They walked for a long time again; and at sunset they drew near a cemetery. At that moment the boy said to Khenge: "Here is my village."

When Khenge realized what was happening to her, she started weeping. But the boy intimidated her by saying: "Keep silent because the inhabitants of the village hate tears." After, he raised a big stone under which there was a whole. Then he told Khenge to come into the hole first. Khenge tried to enter the hole, but the basket she was carrying was obstructing the whole entrance.

Then she proposed this to the boy:" Take my basket and go into the hole; after I'll push the basket from the outside." The boy came into the hole and started pulling the basket. At this moment a dung-beetle came close to Khenge and asked what she was doing. Khenge told the dung-beetle the circumstances.

The dung-beetle said: "If you go into this hole, you won't certainly get out of it quickly. Let me push the basket on behalf of you and as for you, take advantage of this opportunity and flee away. "

The dung-beetle gave Khenge a magic object which enabled her to fly. It replaced Khenge at the whole entrance. Meanwhile, the boy did not notice this stratagem and kept on shouting: "Khenge, will you push the basket?"

The dung-beetle, imitating Khenge's voice, replied: "I'm pushing the basket And the boy kept on pulling the basket; but it was resisting. At last, the dung-beetle pushed it so strongly that it came into the hole. Then the boy called out: Khenge, come in quickly!"

But, as Khenge no longer answered, the boy became anxious, got out of the hole and saw nobody. The dung-beetle had, in turn, flown away. The boy attempted to pursue Khenge but did not catch her up. Khenge had come back to her parents' home and told them what had happened to her.

Her mother gave her the following counsel: "From now on, know that the choice of a mate depends neither on beauty nor on smartness, but on some qualities and aptitudes. That's why one of our proverbs says: Before eating a piece of fruit, first inform yourself about the tree from which it had been picked up."

QUESTIONS AND EXERCISES

I. True or False? Justify your answer
1. Khenge was a meek girl.
2. Khenge was considerate to other people.
3. Khenge did not want to marry a perfect boy.
4. Khenge and the boy fell in love at first sight.
5. Khenge was rescued miraculously.
6. When Khenge came back home her mother did not tell her anything.

II: Find in the tale phrases which mean the following
1. Khenge used to treat other people with contempt.
2. She wanted to get married with someone who had no physical deficiencies.
3. Khenge and the boy looked fixedly at each other amorously.
4. The young boy told Khenge to bring all her things of value.
5. The young boy got rid of his shirt and trousers.
6. The dung-beetle drew near Khenge.
7. The villagers don't like weeping people.

III: Write questions to which these phrases or words are the answers.
1. A pretty girl.
2. To the market.
3. To sell her vegetables.
4. A brown complexion.
5. At the bottom of the market.
6. Longingly
7. That he wanted to marry her
8. At sunset.
9. Khenge's voice.
10. To pursue Khenge.

IV: Discussion points which: statement corresponds best to this tale?
1. Appearances are misleading.
2. Beware of people you don't know.
3. Do not have dealings with people whose qualities, aptitudes and background you ignore.
4. A shrewd person discerns calamities and avoids them.
5. You sometimes need someone smaller than yourself.

V: Imagine a 12 line conversation between Khenge and the boy from the moment they leave the market to their arrival at "the boy's village."

VI: Write a summary of this tale (90 words).

Glossary
Baffled: bemused, confused.
Complexion: the natural color of the skin.
Dazzling: making a strong or vivid impression.
Defectless: without imperfections.
Dung - beetle: a coleopterous insect having a head with horny spikes.
Endowed with: having something by inheritance or nature.
Haughty: arrogant, condescending.
To consider people as base as dogs: to despise people, to treat them with contempt.
To despise: to contempt.
To head for: to go to.

3

CHAPTER

How Langa became a Village Chief

Pre-reading task

From the headline, predict the content of this tale (50 words). Use the words and the phrases in the box

> skilled hunter, sanguinary feuds, chieftaincy function, village, rivals, to get rid of, sole appointee, to break out, squabbles of succession

Langa was a skilled hunter because he used to supply his village with a lot of varied meat of animals he had captured. He was famous and enjoyed a good reputation both inside and outside his village.

In the course of the time, Kabe, the village chief, became old and unable to discharge correctly his functions. As he was about to die, the peaceful village fell into unremitting squabbles of succession. In fact, Kabe had many wives and a great number of children. Each of the wives wanted one of her sons to become the village chief. That is why long and sanguinary feuds broke out among the sons of Kabe.

Once, as Langa was coming from hunting, he met a Leopard. He at first was frightened. But, the animal did not display any aggressiveness and a quarrelsome behavior: it was simply searching for something to eat. The Leopard asked the hunter to give it some meat and, in compensation, promised to help him. The hunter agreed. On the following day Langa came back where he had encountered the Leopard and gave it some more meat. From that day on, Langa and the Leopard regularly met many times. They became close friends. That is why the Leopard became Langa's confidante; Langa kept the animal informed on the intrigues and quarrels about Kabe's succession.

Upon hearing this, the Leopard told the hunter that it would be of a great assistance to him. It suggested telling both the village elders and the villagers to leave the village for one night without Kabe's sons knowing it.

That is why, one night, some Leopards penetrated into the village and devoured all those who were claiming for the chieftaincy function .And so, they could help Langa get rid of all his rivals; and Langa remained the sole appointee to the chieftaincy function.

As the villagers were appreciating him because of his generosity and strength, this explains why, some days later, after Kabe's death, the Board of Elders appointed Langa Chief of the village.

QUESTIONS AND EXERCISES
I: True or False? Justify your answer.
1. Langa was unknown in his village.
2. Langa and the Leopard have always been close friends.
3. Langa discovered by his own the stratagem to get rid of Kabe's sons.
4. Kabe's sons were informed about the invasion of the village by some Leopards.
5. Kabe was appointed the village chief by all the villagers.

II: Use the words in the box to fill in the gaps.

appointee   board   confidante   elders   feud   function   squabbles

1. The---------------------of a teacher is to give a good education to students.
2. Yesterday a violent------------------broke out between these two bands.
3. ----------are considered reservoirs of knowledge in many African societies.
4. Ngugi trusts fully Ilunga because he can tell him secrets and open his mind to him. That is why Ilunga is Ngugi's-----------
5. The members of this college have just elected their--------------of education.
6. A peace agreement has been signed between these communities to put an end to their permanent---------

III: Put these sentences in the correct order.
1. The village fell into unremitting squabbles of succession.
2. The Leopard and Langa regularly met.
3. Langa was appointed the village chief by the elders.
4. Langa was a skilled hunter.
5. Langa came from the forest and met the Leopard.
6. Kabe became old and unable to discharge his functions.
7. The leopard suggested helping Langa.
8. Some leopards invaded the village and devoured all Langa's rivals.

1. Langa used	a-her sons to be at the head of the village
2. Each of the women wanted	b-because he was very generous
3. The leopard proposed	c-to help Langa
4. The villagers loved Langa	d-to provide the village with a lot of meat
5. The leopard suggested that village, except	e-all the villagers should leave the Kabe's sons.

V: **Collocations. Vocabulary**

Find two of the phrases on the right which go with the five verbs on the left.

1. To meet	a. a rival
2. To fall	b aggressiveness
3. To suggest	c. a stratagem
4. To display	d. on hunting
5. To keep	e. into intrigues
	f. to leave the village
	g. someone informed of a situation
	h. into sanguinary feuds
	I. a quarrelsome behavior
	j. a friend

VI: What do you think?

To get rid of Langa's rivals, the Leopard and Langa have acted:

a) Unscrupulously
b) Kindly
c) Wickedly
d) Cynically
e) Honestly
f) Righteously

Elicit your choice

VII-Make a summary of this tale (90 words)

Glossary

Appointee: someone who has been established officially for a
          position.
Board: a governing and organized body.
Confidante: a trusted friend, secrets and private matters can be
          disclosed to him/her.
Feud: a state of enmity punctuated with violent conflicts.
Skilled: very qualified, very well trained, experienced.
Sole: unique.
Squabble: noisy quarrel.
Unremitting: persistent.

4

CHAPTER

Two Orphans

Pre-reading task

-Ask 5 questions from the two first paragraphs. Go from "Two orphans"
"to and said."
-Predict the content of the tale (60 words).

Two orphans were living in a village. The eldest one was a pirogue man. He owned a knife and used it to fight aquatic animals. The youngest one used to set traps and to catch only small animals; but he had never succeeded in keeping animals in his traps. As he had nothing to build more solid traps with, one day, he took his brother's knife and went into the forest.

There he caught a rat and an antelope. And he found a boar in a trap trying to escape. Then he drew his brother's knife out of its holster and stabbed the boar. The boar succeeded in extricating itself from the trap and fled away. Unable to tackle this situation, the boy came back home with the animals he had captured and told his brother the circumstances. The latter became angry and said:

"Give me back my knife. I shan't accept any other one." As he could not meet his brother's requirements, the young boy went back to the forest and approached a river. There he saw a crocodile which asked him this question: "What are you looking for, young boy?"

The boy replied: "I am looking for the boar which had fled away with my brother's knife."

The crocodile replied: "First of all, clean my scales thoroughly and I'll tell you what you'll have to do."

The boy accepted to clean the scales thoroughly. Then the crocodile said: "There is a case near here. Go there and knock at the first door."

The boy obeyed. When the door opened, he saw a human monster, a woman, with very long hair. The monster said: "Stay where you are; if you go away, you will die."

The boy stayed still and erect; and the monster asked him: "Who sent you here?"

The boy answered: "It was the crocodile; I told it the story about my brother's knife. I have stabbed the boar I had caught in a trap and the boar had fled away with the knife."

The woman asked the boy to cut off her long hair. The boy did so. Then the monster said: "Not far from here there is one door. This door paves the way to an underground room. Go there, open it and get into the room."

The boy did what he had been told and entered the room. There he saw a lot of half-naked women. As soon as they saw him, the women jumped of joy and said: "What a good surprise! From now on we'll have someone to cook our food." The boy stayed with the women for many days, cooking and doing all the household chores.

One day, the oldest woman asked him why he had come there. The boy told her the story about his brother's knife. The woman gave him one knife and three eggs and said to him: "You will break down the first egg on the ground, and, as a result, you will return home miraculously. And when you are at home, break down the second egg, and then you will see around you a large town full of people of all origins. Finally, you will break down the third egg and you will become a town chief."

The boy followed obediently the woman's instructions; and all the woman's predictions were realized. The boy became the chief of a town.

After that, he entrusted his eldest brother with important responsibilities in the town. Unfortunately, the eldest boy puffed up with pride, started to behave in an unacceptable manner towards the town inhabitants: he used to be rude towards them and uncouth in his dealings with them. On hearing that, the town chief sacked him and inflicted a punishment on him.

The eldest brother became angry and furious and took the decision of leaving the town. He, in turn, approached a river and met a crocodile. The crocodile asked him what he was looking for. He said that, like his brother, he wanted to become a town chief.

The crocodile said:"If you clean my scales out, I'll be in a position to reveal you a secret which will enable you to become a town chief in your turn." The boy rejected this proposal. Nevertheless, the crocodile pointed to a case, told him to go there and to knock at the case door. The boy did so, and a human monster opened the door.

After welcoming him, the monster enquired about the reason of his visit. The boy said that, like his youngest brother, he was targeting to become a town chief.

The monster replied: "If you want to realize your ambition, start by cutting off my hair." The boy rejected this request flatly. Then, the monster led him to an underground room. There, like his youngest brother, he encountered a lot of half naked women who welcomed him.

The oldest woman gave him three eggs and told him to break them off according to predetermined order.

The boy broke down the first egg and was miraculously hurled into his home. Once there, instead of breaking down the second egg, he broke down the third one. And as a result, he was suddenly surrounded by all sorts of animals. And when he broke down the third egg, a great fire came down from heaven and burnt him down.

QUESTIONS AND EXERCISES
I: True or false? Justify your answer.
1. The two boys had different parents.
2. The two boys were doing the same job.
3. The youngest boy went into the forest at the request of his eldest brother.
4. When the youngest boy saw the human monster, he was very pleased.
5. At first, the monster told the youngest brother to cook some food.
6. The youngest brother met the crocodile twice.
7. The half naked women were living in an underground room.
8. The oldest women told the boys to eat the eggs.
9. Both boys became town chiefs.
10. The oldest boy remained alive.

II. Use the words in the box and fill the gaps

> -orphans - human -aquatic -trap - river - sacked -underground -pirogue man

1. Whales live under water. They are------------------------------ mammals.
2. Uhuru uses a small pirogue to help people cross the river. He is a----------------------
3. Katala and Umba have lost their parents. They are--------------
4. To go to the other side of the street safely, these pupils have to go through an-------passage.
5. Our house is infested with mice. We must use a---------------- to catch them.
6. Last week this managing director--------his workers because they had been on strike for a long time.
7. A----------------------separates the two parts of this town.

III: Put these sentences in the correct order

1. The youngest boy came close to a river.
2. The boar extricated itself from the trap and fled away.
3. The youngest boy caught a rat and an antelope in a forest.
4. The youngest boy caught a boar in a trap.
5. Two orphans were living in a village.
6. The crocodile told the eldest boy to clean its scales thoroughly.
7. The crocodile told the eldest boy to go to a case.
8. A human monster told the youngest boy to cut off his long hair.
9. The youngest boy went back to the forest.

IV: Discussion points: which sentences correspond best to this tale? Explain

1. Being humble is more preferable than being haughty.
2. Heeding instructions is more beneficial than ignoring them.
3. All is well that ends well.
4. Anger can lead to dire consequences.

V: Make a summary of this tale (80 words).

Glossary

Boar: male pig.

Chore: boring, routine activity, unpleasant task in a house.

Flatly: firmly and definitely.

Frightened: feeling fear.

Household: domestic task in connection with the management of a house.

Naked: wearing no clothes, having no clothing on the body.

Orphan: a child whose parents are dead.

Pirogue man: someone who uses pirogues to transport people from one side of a river to the other side.

Prediction: foretold event which will be realized in the future.

Requirement: something which should be done.

Rude: impolite.

Scales: small hard flat pieces on the skin of a crocodile, a snake............

To entrust someone with responsibilities: to assign someone some specific tasks and duties.

To pave the way to: to indicate the direction to a place.

To sack: to dismiss someone from a job.

To stab: to pierce, to wound with a knife.

To tackle a situation: to handle a situation, to deal with a situation.

Trap: object used for catching animals.

Uncouth: unpleasant.

5

CHAPTER

The Ogre and the Boy

Pre-reading task

Give related ideas or vocabulary in connection with the word **"ogre"**

Predict the content of the tale by using the words in the box (50 words)

-song -to swallow -to eat -bush   -beans -hiding place

A man and a woman had a boy. An ogre called *Ntumba Kansensa* was living in the village. That is why whenever they went into the forest to work in their field, they locked up their boy in their house, and they barricaded the house door with tree trunks and gave the boy the following recommendation: "If the ogre comes here and calls you, do not open him the door."

One day, when they left home, the ogre came singing and said to the boy:

> *"Oh boy, open me the door*
> *So I can come into your house*
> *Poor of me, Ntumba Kansensa, the whimperer*
> *If you don't want me to swallow you*
> *Give me some beans so I can eat them*

Upon hearing this song, the boy was frightened and opened the door. The ogre came into the house, took some beans and ate them voraciously. The boy, staying motionless and tense, glanced at him timidly. Then the ogre left the house. When the boy's parents came back from the forest, the boy told them what had occurred. They expressed discontent and swore to get rid of the ogre. That is why, after feigning going to the forest, they, in fact, hid behind a bush near their house.

Taking advantage of this situation, the ogre came back again and acted as the first time he had come to the house: he sang and threatened to swallow the boy in case he didn't open him the door. While he was about to enter the house, the boy's parents left their hiding place, rushed quickly to the ogre. And the man shot him dead with a rifle. Then he threw his corpse into a dump.

QUESTIONS AND EXERCISES
I: Comprehension questions:
1. Why did the man and the woman lock up their boy in their house?
2. What was their job?
3. What did the ogre do when he came into the house?
4. How did the boy react?
5. How many times did the ogre come to the house?
6. Were the boy's parents glad when they learned what had happened?
7. How did the ogre finish?

II: Write questions to which the following words or phrases are the answers.

1. In a village
2. In their house
3. Into the forest
4. Some beans
5. Voraciously

III: Match these statements

1.The ogre threatened 2.The man and his wife 3.The ogre ate 4.The boy's parents 5.The boy	a. swore an oath to suppress the ogre b. some beans c. went into the forest to work in their field d. to swallow the boy e. didn't heed his parents' instructions

IV: Match the words in the box with their meanings

-ogre -discontent -beans -dump -to threaten -to glance at corpse -recommendation

1. instruction given to avoid a difficult situation.
2. the body of a dead person.
3. an area into which rubbish is thrown.
4. to menace.
5. to look at quickly.
6. seeds of various plants that are edible after being cooked.
7. a huge and ferocious character.
8. lack of satisfaction.

V: Which statement corresponds best to this tale? Explain.
1. Justice is not always denied.
2. The rights of the strongest do not always prevail.
3. Whoever keeps sowing wind will reap storm wind.
4. Children are advised to take into account their parents' recommendations.

VI: Write one sentence to summarize each paragraph.

Glossary

Hiding place: hideout, place where someone can hide

Oath: formal promise

Tense: anxious and nervous

To barricade: to close off with a barrier, a bulwark

To lock up: to put someone, something in a safe place fastened by a lock.

To swear-swore-sworn: to declare officially and solemnly, to give one's word.

Whimperer: someone who weeps with a broken and mournful tone.

CHAPTER

A Hunter's Woman and a Dog

Pre-reading task
Give related ideas to the words 'hunter' and 'dog'
Predict the content of this tale (50 words) by using the words in the box

> -fish   -bush -cassava leaves -to cook -puppy -to catch

There were once a hunter, his wife and a dog. They were living in a village. The hunter and his wife ate neither cooked cassava leaves nor other vegetables. They usually ate fish called *Misangi* which the man had caught from a river and the meat of animals he had captured from hunting.

One day the man went to the river. Coming back from there with a lot of *Misangi*, he gave them to his wife and said: "My dear wife, if you cook this fish, eat your share and leave me mine." After that, he went hunting. His wife stayed home, roasted the fish, ate them and left nothing for her husband.

When he came back home, he claimed for his share of the *Misangi*. His wife said that, while he was absent, their dog had eaten all the fish. On hearing that, the hunter took a bludgeon to hit the dog. But the latter replied immediately by singing as follows:

*"Oh! The hunter's wife is a liar
It's her who had eaten her husband's Misangi
Now she is pretending that it's her puppy which had eaten
them.
Poor of me, at present my stomach is empty
It's quite empty the stomach of the puppy."*

After listening to this song, the hunter realized what had occurred, got boiling mad but controlled his anger. That is why on another day, before going hunting, he gave again some fish to his wife. She roasted them once more, ate them all without leaving anything for him.

When he came back and claimed for his share, his woman answered: "It's your puppy which had eaten your share." The hunter took a stick and, while he was raising his hands to hit the dog, the latter stopped him and sang as previously. On hearing this song, the hunter refrained from hitting the dog. To clarify this situation, he resorted to a stratagem: he gave again his wife a lot of fish and told her that he will be going round a faraway bush. In reality he hid in a nearby bush.

From his hiding place he kept observing his wife. He saw her roasting the fish and eating them gluttonously with some food. She left nothing for him. After that, the hunter left the bush and feigned asking for his share of the fish. But, as usual, his wife lied. The hunter rushed impetuously to her and struck her with a stick. While he was doing that, he said to her, "your lies deserve a correction of this kind."

QUESTIONS AND EXERCISES

I. True or false? Justify.

1. The hunter and his wife were vegetarians.

2. The dog behaved like a human being.

3. The hunter's wife was honest with her husband.

4. The hunter went to hide near a river.

5. After the hunter had discovered his wife's treachery, he forgave her.

II. Match the words on the left with their meanings on the right

1. Hunter	a. to tell a false statement
2. Bludgeon	b. roots that can be cooked and transformed into flour
3. Cassava	
4. Puppy	c. a heavy-headed stick used to strike people with
5. Hiding place	
	d. a safe place from where you can't be seen
6. To roast	e. to cook above a fire
7. To feign	f. to make semblance of doing something
8. To lie	g. very young dog
	h. someone who chases wild animals

III: Fill the gaps using the right verbs.

1. To----------------cassava leaves

2. To---------------the fish

3. To--------------a bludgeon

4. To--------------from hitting the dog

5. To----------------in a bush

IV. Complete these sentences:

1. The hunter and his woman------------------------------------

2. The man caught---

3. After roasting the fish, the hunter's woman--------------------

4. After realizing what t had occurred, the hunter---------------

5. The hunter came back from hunting and----------------------

V: Discussion points: which statement corresponds best to this tale?
1. Lying is not always beneficial
2. Liars are not trustworthy people
3. It is allowed to lie from time to time
4. What you are really will be discovered some day

VI: Write a summary of this tale (70 words)

VII: Imagine a continuation to this tale (40 words)

Glossary
Anger: fury, indignation, wrath
Bludgeon: a stout heavy club. It is small, thicker and loaded
          at end.
Gluttonously: without self-control, with greediness
Harmlessness: Innocence
Liar: Someone who does not speak the truth
Lie: a saying which is not true
Previously: before
To deserve: to merit
To feign: to make semblance of
To get boiling mad: to become very furious, to be hopping mad
To refrain from: to prevent from

7
CHAPTER

A Hunter, his Wife and their Dog

Pre-reading task

What is a:
a) Protest song?
b) Troublesome situation?

From the headline, predict the content of the tale (40 words)
A hunter and his wife were living in a village called *Mulamba Lungandu.* They had many children. Whenever the hunter went hunting, he took a gun. One day, he said to his wife:"As I usually go hunting far away and as I have no dog, it would be better for me to buy one. For in case a wild animal attacks me, the dog can bark, be menacing and make the animal flee away."

After that, the hunter went to another village to buy a dog. The dog's name was Bulungu and was very useful to him: it helped him catch a lot of animals. One day, as his gunpowder faded away, the hunter took his bicycle and went hunting without his gun. He left his wife, children and dog at home.

At meal time, the hunter's wife, instead of giving food to the dog, threw it on the floor and said:

"You dirty puppy, I am not your Master.
Who loves you as if you were a human being.
As if you were his child.
Now take in your food."

As a sign of protest, the dog disagreed to eat and started intoning
the following song:

"Oh my Master, if you want to give me something.
Do not speak about it with your wife.
The women of the village Mulamba Lungandu are odd.
Your own wife has thrown my food on the floor.
Saying that I am only a dog.
Poor of me Bulungu.
From now on I'll go back to my parents' country.
Where food is as white as kaolin
Where food is well appreciated
Where it is cut with some needles
Where it is cooked with some small iron bars
Where white people eat tender leaves of beans
And where black people eat mushrooms."

The dog went away chanting the same song. It was heard by a lot
of people. And after crisscrossing a large area, the dog approached
a river and crossed it. When it arrived near a large grove, it met
its master. The latter was surprised and questioned," Is this dog
mine or of anyone else?"

He got off his bicycle, took his dog in both hands and went
back home. Once at home, he asked his wife to tell him what
she had done towards the dog. But before she replied, the dog
intoned the protest song again and this time loudlier.The wife
uttered some words trying to prove that she had not behaved
towards the dog as a misdoer. The hunter exclaimed: "What a
troublesome situation!" Finally, he slapped her and dismissed

her, saying: "Now go back to your parents' home and open your ears to their counsels. You do need it."

QUESTIONS AND EXERCISES

I: Choose the right answer

1. The hunter and his wife
   a) were childless
   b) had one boy
   c) were a big family

2. The hunter wanted to buy a dog because
   a) he loved dogs
   b) he thought a dog would be useful to him
   c) he wanted a second dog

3. The hunter's wife was
   a) Considerate towards dogs.
   b) Contemptuous towards the dog.
   c) Full of empathy with the dog.

4. The dog met its master
   a) not far from a grove
   b) in the middle of a river
   c) near a large grove

5. The hunter
   a) left the dog in the river
   b) followed the dog
   c) went back home with the dog

II: Match the statements in Table A with those in Table B

TABLE A	TABLE B
1. The hunter	a. that she did not love the dog
2. The hunter wanted	b. intoning a protest song
3. The hunter's wife showed	c. to protect himself against
4. The dog started	wild animals
5. The hunter decided	d. to dismiss his wife
	e. usually goes hunting
	faraway

III: Complete these gaps with words from the tale
1. s-------------------of p----------------s------------------
2. g-----------p----------------d------------r
3. h---------------a-------------b------------------n---------
4. l----------------------v----------of b-----------n---------
5. m--------------sh----------------------m-----------------

IV: Correct these statements
1. The hunter and his wife had three dogs.
2. The hunter and his wife were living in an unknown village.
3. The hunter's wife gave the dog some food at meal time.
4. The dog met its master in the middle of a river.
5. The dog chanted a song praising the hunter's wife.

VI: Put these sentences in the correct order
1. The hunter went to another village to buy a dog.
2. The dog met its master near a large grove.
3. The hunter and his wife had many children.
4. The dog started intoning a protest song.
5. The hunter went back home with the dog.
6. The hunter and his wife were living in a village.
7. The hunter left his wife, children and dog at home.
8. The hunter left the village.
9. The hunter's wife threw the dog's food on the floor.

VII: Discussion points

A: Choose the right answer and explain
This tale deals with problems of:
a. Honesty
b. Dignity
c. Hypocrisy
d. Lying
e. Treachery

B: Which statement corresponds best to this tale? Explain.
1. You cannot conceal permanently what you are really.
2. Having insight greatly contributes greatly avoiding calamities.

Glossary
Grove: a group of trees planted close together.
Insight: perspicacity.
Kaolin: fine white clay.
Misdoere: someone who has carried out a bad action.
Needle: a thin pointed bar used in sewing.
Odd: abnormal, bizarre.
To crisscross: to go across.
To run out: to diminish in quantity.
To take in: to swallow.

CHAPTER

The Robber of Bananas

Pre-reading task
Predict ten words or phrases that can appear in this tale
Use the words in the box to predict the content of this tale (30 words)

> -pineapples -sugar canes -banana bunch -owner   -field

A man called Mamba had a large field in the forest. He planted in it all sorts of crops: pineapples, sugar canes, carrots, cassava, bananas, plantains, groundnuts, etc. As this field had often been robbed, *Mamba* decided to hire some guards and to keep himself a close watch on it. Despite these protective measures, he had never been in a position to catch the robber. One day a robber came to the field and said cynically: "As usual, I'll stockpile some bananas from the field."

He rooted out carrots and cassava, cut down some sugar canes and pineapples. After that he went to a river, drew near a banana tree and attempted to cut down a banana bunch. When he took his machete, he heard the banana bunch singing as follows:

"Oh, my master, don't cut me down yet.
Me, a drum emitting enrapturing sounds.

Upon hearing the banana bunch singing, the robber started to dance; he danced a lot for a long time. Finally, he raised his machete and said: "Now I must absolutely finish my job with this banana bunch which had made me dance so much."

As he was poised to give the blow to the bunch, the latter moved to another place singing endlessly. The robber stood up and danced again until night time. Then darkness occurred, surprised him and preventing him from going back home.

That is why he decided to sleep there, under the mysterious banana tree. He woke up in the next morning and said: "Before the field owner arrives I have to cut down this banana bunch which had constrained me to spend the whole night here."

As soon as he raised his machete, the banana bunch sang once again. The robber became dazzled and kept on dancing without interruption. At that moment Mamba arrived; and when he saw the robber dancing, he exclaimed: "My Goodness, I have been looking for the robber for a long time! And now who is that who is dancing amid my bananas, my sugar canes, my carrots and my cassava leaves?" Then he moved slowly and stealthily towards the robber. The latter noticed nothing and the field owner caught him.

QESTIONS AND EXERCISES

I: Answer the following questions:
1. What did Mamba plant in his field?
2. Which measures did he take to protect his field?
3. What did the robber do when he came to the field?
4. How did the banana bunch react when the robber tried to cut it down?
5. What does the song reveal about Mamba?
6. What did the robber do when he heard the banana tree singing?
7. Where did the robber sleep?
8. Did the field owner cry when he caught the robber?

II: Make true sentences:

Mamba The robber	1. drew near a banana tree
	2. danced until night time
	3. raised his machete to cut down the banana bunch
	4. hired some guards
	5. had a large field
	6. went to a river
	7. caught the robber unobtrusively
	8. started to dance

III: Find phrases in the tale that mean the following:
1. He possessed a large arable land.
2. He had never been able to capture the burglar.
3. He came close to a tree producing bananas.
4. He was poised to cut down the banana bunch.
5. He took the decision of using the services of some paid custodians.
6. Then he went unhurriedly and furtively into the direction of the robber.

IV. Discussion points: which statement corresponds best to this tale? Explain:

1. Avoid being naive and foolhardy in life.
2. Do not allow any event to distract you from your priorities.
3. Let us cultivate shrewdness: it can allow us to discern dangerous situations and to avoid them.

V: Write a summary of this tale (90 words).

VI: Imagine a continuation to this tale (50 words).

Glossary

Foolhardy: silly, taking unnecessary risks.
Navel: the small sunken mark in the region of the abdomen.
Robber: someone who steals.
Shrewdness: perspicacity.
Stealthily: without making any noise, with discretion.
To be poised to: to be about to.
To burgle: to steal from a building after breaking into it.
To stockpile: to collect.

9

CHAPTER

A Boy and a Man with a naked chest

Pre-reading task

Fill the gaps with the words in the box

> -waved   -bride price -goats   -edge   -whimpered   -prostrate
> -broke loose -chest

1. The boy's father offered his son some------------- as presents.
2. The goats -------- ---------- in the middle of the forest.
3. Before he gets married, this man must pay a ---------------------
   to his family-in-law.
4. Very saddened by his father's death, this boy lay----------- at
   the ----------- of the road.
5. After losing all his presents, the boy-----------------.
6. The man with a naked -----------------his arms triumphantly.

A man had a boy who wanted to get married when he reached adulthood. That is why he offered the boy some goats to allow him to pay a bride price. The boy took the goats and left home. When he arrived in the middle of a bush, the goats broke loose and fled away. The boy ran after them and could not recapture them. Prostrate, he sat down at the edge of a road and wept bitterly.

At this moment a man with a naked chest came suddenly out of the bush and said to the boy: "What would you offer me if I helped you recapture the goats?" The boy replied: "I'll do whatever you want." The man went into the bush and, after a while, came back with all the goats.

Then he said to the boy: "I'll accompany you wherever you'll go to look for your wife." If, at our arrival, people welcome us by saying: "Welcome to both of you, each present that will be offered to us will be mine." If, on the contrary, people welcome us by saying: "Welcome to you boy, every present that will be offered will be yours." The boy accepted this deal .As soon as they arrived at the home of the boy's prospective family-in-law, everybody hurried up shouting: "Welcome to both of you, honorable visitors."

Immediately the man with a naked chest waved his arms triumphantly and took all the presents that were offered to them: food, meat and a lot of other presents. On their way back home with the boy's wife, they arrived in the middle of the bush.

There, the man with a naked chest said to the boy: "Now let us share equitably what remains for you."

The boy gave him all the meat he had intended to bring to his father. And at the same moment, several men with naked chests rushed out of the bush, claiming for their shares of the presents. They grabbed the woman, prevented the boy from going home with her.

Realizing what was happening to him, incapable of reversing the dreadful course of the events, the boy whimpered and returned home empty-handed.

QUESTIONS

I. Choose the right answer.

1. To allow his boy to pay the bride price, the man offered him:
    a) some money
    b) some animals
    c) some valuables

2. The goats broke loose:
    a) near a bush
    b) in the middle of a forest
    c) in the core of the bush

3. When the goats fled away, the boy was:
    a) overwhelmed with grief
    b) very nervous
    c) panic-stricken

4. The goats were recaptured by:
    a) the boy
    b) the man with a naked chest
    c) men with naked chests

5. When the boy and the man with a naked chest reached the home of the boy's wife:
    a) people welcomed them with songs
    b) people welcomed them warmly and honorably
    c) people fell upon their necks and kissed them

6. The man with a naked chest:
    a) shared all the presents with the boy
    b) gave some presents to the boy
    c) shared no presents with the boy

II. Fill the gaps using the words in the box

> - adulthood - goats -bride price - chest -naked-bitterly - presents
> - prostrate

1. This shepherd is unable to make a distinction between
   ------- and sheep.
2. When a child is born, he is-------------
3. The-------------of this statue is in bronze and its legs are in gold.
4. Mary was--------------when she learned her uncle's death.
5. In some countries you needn't pay a---------------------before
   getting married.
6. Susan didn't appreciate these--------- because they were awful.
7. This football coach accepted the defeat of his team-------------
8. Peter can't have a driving license because he is 12 years old.
   He has not reached----- yet.

III. Put these sentences in the correct order.

1. The goats broke loose and fled away.
2. The man with a naked chest recaptured the goats.
3. The boy expressed the desire   of getting married.
4. The boy took the goats and went away.
5. A man with a naked chest emerged.
6. The men with naked chests grabbed the woman and prevented
   the boy from bringing her home.
7. They received some presents.
8. Some men with naked chests came out of the bush.
9. On their way back home they arrived in the middle of a
   bush.
10. The boy and the man with a naked chest were welcomed
    by the people.

IV. Discussion points: which statement corresponds best to this tale?

1. It is unwise to trust someone you do not know.
2. We must take time to reflect before making promises.
3. We needn't make inconsiderate promises.
4. You needn't go back on your promises even when things
   become bad for you.

V. Write a summary of this tale (90 words).

*VI. Imagine a continuation to this tale in the form of a 12-line
   dialogue between the boy and his father.*

Glossary
Bride price: dowry, money or property brought by a bridegroom
            to his bride before his marriage.
Chest: thorax, the upper part of a human body.
Dreadful: awful, terrible.
Proposal: offer, deal.

Prostrate: undergoing extreme weakness.
To break loose: to escape.
To rush out of: to get out suddenly from.
To whimper: to weep with broken plaintive sounds.

10
CHAPTER

Two Boys and their Mothers

Pre-reading task

Ask five questions about the three first paragraphs.

Two young boys who were getting along well decided to go and live in a bush far from their village. At the beginning of the rainy season they decided to erect huts as shelters for their respective mothers. The first boy finished building his mother's hut; the second did not do so.

One day, as it started raining heavily, the second boy asked the first one to shelter his mother for a limited period of time; the latter replied: "In any case, I don't want your mother to live with mine." Disappointed, the second boy climbed a tree called *Lusanga* and installed his mother there. Meanwhile, it got on raining abundantly all night.

The second boy stood under a tree, fearing that his mother might be carried away by the wind. After a while, it stopped raining and the weather became mild. The next day in the morning, the second boy climbed the tree and found his mother dead. He mourned her very heavily, descended her corpse and put it into a game bag he had manufactured with veins cut from some palm trees.

While he was doing this, the first boy was observing him without saying any word. Then, the second boy took his mother's corpse, went away weeping bitterly and singing as follows:

> *"My poor mother*
> *Little tom-tom producing wonderful sounds*
> *She had been carried away*
> *By a thundery shower*
> *Little tom-tom producing wonderful sounds*
> *Who used to uproot the stumps of trees*
> *Little tom producing wonderful sounds."*

The boy went across two villages. At his arrival in the third village, he kept on singing. Then, he went into a thick grass bush and heard someone calling him:

You boy, come and clean my eyes. For know that all those who had cleaned my eyes have not undergone death "The boy threw a glance at the area from which the voice was coming and saw an old woman. Then he said: "Why are you calling me? Do you think that I am able to clean your nauseating eyes?"

Finally, the boy took his courage in both hands, put his game bag on the floor, came close to the woman and cleaned her eyes. When he finished cleaning them, the old woman said: "Listen, young boy, where you will go, you'll find two ponds. One with stagnant waters, another with running water. You will hear from the last pond voices saying:

"Give us something to eat; do not throw your mother's corpse into this pond. On the contrary, throw it into the pond with stagnant waters. Follow these recommendations and you will see what will happen. May God protect you."

The young boy pursued his way singing. He reached a forest where he found the two ponds. Then he heard voices saying: "Give us something to eat. Give us something to eat."

He came close to the pond with stagnant waters and threw his mother's corpse into it. After that, a very pretty girl got out of the pond. She had with her a brand new car full of valuable items. She said to the boy: "Don't panic, I am your wife. Come into the car and let's go home."

The boy agreed. When they reached their home, a court, the young woman, with a magic gesture, made the court very clean. When she performed another magic gesture, a lot of workers appeared suddenly and filled the court. The young boy was dazzled. And as for the first boy who was observing this scene in silence, he was covered with shame. Full of rage, he knocked out his mother to death with a cudgel, made a game bag, put his mother's corpse into it and went away. He was, in his turn, called by the old woman who asked him to clean her eyes. The boy replied: "Oh, you villain, go to the devil. Who are you to ask me to clean your eyes? Do you think you are in a position to be compared with my mother I have just knocked out?"

The old woman said nothing. The boy went on until he arrived at the pond with stagnant waters. Then he heard voices saying: "Give us something to eat, give us something to eat." As a reply, he threw his mother's corpse into the pond. And some time later, an old woman, older than his mother, came out of the pond. When he saw her, he jumped up furiously towards her, struck her to death with a cudgel and threw her corpse into the pond .And so; he lost both his own mother and the old woman who had been offered to him.

QUESTIONS

I. Answer the following questions:

1. What did the two boys do to shelter their mothers?
2. What did the second boy do when he found his mother dead?
3. What did he do with his mother's corpse?
4. What had the boy used to manufacture the game bag?
5. What did he hear when he reached a thick grass bush?
6. Where did the second boy throw his mother's corpse?
7. What happened after?
8. Where did the boy and the girl go?
9. What did the pretty girl do?
10. What happened after?

II. Find phrases in the tale that mean the following:

1. Two boys were on good terms.
2. I don't want your mother to live with mine.
3. The boy reached the top of a tree.
4. The boy was looking at him in silence.
5. The old woman didn't open her mouth.
6. The boy rushed towards her angrily.

III. Find the opposites of the following words and phrases:

1. Young:	6. To come close to:
2. Far:	7. Rainy season
3. Boy:	8. Wonderful:
4. Thick:	9. Death:
5. Long:	10. Brand new:

IV. Fill the gaps with some words from the tale:

1. This policeman used a------------------to hit this demonstrator.
2. These people took---------------from the air raids in the
    underground.
3. Peter wrote an interesting book last year. It was--------------
    documented.
4. The weather is generally wet in the-------------------season.
5. There is a---------------full of toads in this park.
6. Whenever he goes hunting, this man carries his----------------
7. When he was contradicted, the manager -------------glanced at
his contradictor.

V. Put these sentences in the correct order:

1. The second boy climbed a tree and found his mother dead.
2. The second boy asked the first boy to shelter his mother for a
    limited period of time.
3. The second boy took away his mother's corpse.
4. The second boy knocked out his mother to death.
5. The second boy descended his mother's corpse from the tree.
6. The first boy threw the old lady's corpse into the pond.
7. The first boy finished building his mother's hut.
8. The boys built shelters for their mothers at the beginning of
    the rainy season.
9. The two boys were getting along well.
10. The second boy met an old woman in a thick grass bush.

VI. Discussion points:
1. Anger and arrogance can be harmful.
2. Children have to respect and to honor their parents.
3. Being hospitable can be of a great advantage.
4. Someone who mistreats his parents is causing shame.
5. In life there are constraints we must comply with to get
    success.

VII. Make a summary of this tale (100 words).

Glossary
Cudgel: a stout heavy truncheon. Its end is thick and roundish.
Dazzled: amazed, astonished, stupefied.
Game bag: leather bag.
Pond: a still area of water; it is smaller than a lake.
Shelter: refuge, protection, sanctuary, haven.
Stump: a rooted remnant of a tree.
Too get along well: to be on good terms, to have good
relationships.
To knock out: to hit with a hard blow.
To mourn: to weep with grief and sadness.

CHAPTER

A Woman who killed her Son

Pre-reading task

Fill the gaps with the words in the box

> -palm leaf -assailed -puzzled -forest -yams -bird -moving

1. A small------------was observing the woman silently.
2. The woman and her son went to the--------------------
3. The woman covered the corpse with a small-------- ----------
4. When she saw her son dead, the woman was-----------by fear.
5. They got---------------- to the forest
6. They went to the forest to seek-----------------
7. When she saw her son starting to vomit, the woman was-------

A man called Katala and his wife had a son, Mucowela Ngoyi. The wife regularly went to the forest to seek yams. One day her son asked her: "Mother, can I go with you to the forest to look for yams?" The mother agreed and both of them got moving to the forest.

Once in the forest, the mother dug up a lot of yams, cut them into pieces, put them into a pan and then into a fire. The yams boiled a little and the woman removed them from the fire and gave some pieces to her son. He ate them and started vomiting. A few minutes later, he died.

When she saw that, the woman was assailed by fear and became puzzled. Then, she decided to put her son's corpse onto an anthill and covered it with a small palm leaf. But, while she was doing this, a small bird, staying nearby, was observing her silently.

After covering her son's corpse with the palm leaf, she took her basket, put the remaining yams into it and came back to the village. The bird followed her and started singing as follows:

"Light rain which is falling down
Light rain which is falling down
Poor little Ngoyi
Mucowela Ngoyi
Mucowela son of Katala
Who is lying dead in a bed?
Poor little Ngoyi
Who is covered with a small palm leaf?

Poor little Ngoyi
Mucowela Ngoyi
Whose lips have been twisted?
Poor little Ngoyi
You who are like a mushroom
Poor little Ngoyi
Mucowela Ngoyi."

While the bird was singing, the woman went away, feigning not to hear the bird's song. When she arrived in the village, the bird kept on chanting the same song. As soon as the villagers heard it, they asked the woman where she had left her son. She replied: "My son is coming after me."

This reply shocked them; they became indignant and retorted: "You, cynical woman, are not you jeering at us? You deserve a good correction." Upon hearing this, her husband pounced wrathful upon her and hit her with a stick.

QUESTIONS AND EXERCISES

I: Answer the following questions:

1. Why did the woman regularly go to the forest?
2. What did her son ask her one day?
3. What did the woman do with the yams?
4. What happened to the boy after he had eaten some yams?
5. What did the woman do with her son's corpse?
6. How did the bird help the bird get the woman's treachery discovered?

II: Match the following statements:

1. Katala and his woman-- 2. The woman used-------- 3. The boy-------- 4. After her son's death---- 5. The bird followed--------	a. the woman became frightened and puzzled. b. put some yams into his mouth and started to vomit. c. had a son whose name was Mucowela Ngoyi. d. the woman and started to sing e. to go regularly to the forest to look for some yams.

III: Fill the gaps by using the words in the box:

-son - pan - regularly - puzzled - anthills - corpse - basket -palm

1. There are a lot of--------------in this savannah.
2. This woman is picking some mangoes and is trying to put them into a---------------
3. Peter is Mr. and Mrs. Ngugi's---------------He is 18 years old.
4. John became very------when he saw his brother covered with furuncles from the sole of his feet to his knee cap.

5. The police discovered the boy's------------in an attic yesterday.
6. This lady----------- uses a------------to cook some potatoes.
7. There are some--------------trees in this forest.

IV: Discussion points: which statement corresponds best to this tale?
   Explain.

1. The woman was a cold murderer.
2. After her son's death, the woman did not show an inkling of
   remorse.
3. The woman denied any responsibility in her son's death.
4. The woman killed her son:
   a) Deliberately
   b) Unexpectedly
   c) Accidentally
5. It is unwise to cover our misdemeanours.They will be
   unveiled some day.

V: Write a summary of this tale. (90 words).

VI: Imagine a continuation to this tale (50 words).

Glossary
Indignant: filled with exasperation, angry because of something
          unjust.
Inkling: Slight indication.
Puzzled: filled with perplexity, at a loss.
To be twisted: to be bent into an abnormal shape
To feign: to make semblance of
To jeer at: to laugh derisively at.
To pounce upon: to rush at, to jump on.
To retort: to reply angrily and britally.

SECTION B

ANSWERS TO SOME QUESTIONS AND EXERCISES

Chapter 1: Bindu and the calabash

I .Choice of right answers:
  1. b
  2. c
  3. b
  4. c
  5. c
  6. c

II. Matching words with their definitions.
  1. e
  2. b
  3. g
  4. c
  5. a
  6. f
  7. d

*III. Matching statements in table **A** with those in table **B.***
  1. c
  2. a
  3. b
  4. d
  5. e

IV. Put the statements in the correct order.
  5. 4. 6. 2. 3. 7. 9. 10. 1

V. Finding phrases in the tale

  1. We are terribly hungry.
  2. Bindu forbade his woman to report this story to anyone.
  3. Bindu carried the calabash and went back to the village.
  4. Bindu's wife didn't follow this instruction.
  5. Bindu wrapped the stone in a loincloth.

Chapter 2: A haughty Girl

I. True or false?
1. False. She was an insolent and self-assured girl.
2. False. She was arrogant and disdainful.
3. False. She wanted to marry a boy who was defectless.
4. True. When they met for the first time, they stared at each other amorously.
5. True. A dung-beetle offered her a magic object which allowed her to fly and to be rescued from the young boy's clutches.
6. False. She advised her to be very cautious and very careful in the choice of a mate.

II. Finding phrases in the tale:
1. She used to despise other people, to look at them as base as dogs
2. She wanted to marry a boy who was defectless
3. They stared at each other longingly
4. The boy asked her to get all her valuable items
5. The young boy threw his shirt and trousers away
6. The dung-beetle came close to Khenge
7. Khenge became frightened
8. The inhabitants of this village hate tears

III.Writing questions :
1. What was Khenge like?
2. Where did Khenge go one day?
3. Why did Khenge go to the market?
4. What did the young boy have?
5. Where did Khenge meet the boy?
6.   How did Khenge and the boy stare at each other?
7. What did the boy tell Khenge?
8. When did Khenge and the boy arrive at the cemetery?
9. What did the dung-beetle try to imitate?
10. What did the young boy try/attempt to do?

Chapter 3: How Langa became a village chief

I. True or false? Justification:
    1. False.He was famous and enjoyed a good reputation.
    2. False. They have been closed friends after a lot of meetings.
    3. False. The leopard suggested him this stratagem.
    4. False. They did not know it.
    5. False. He was appointed by the elders.

II. Filling in the gaps:
    1. function
    2. feud
    3. elders
    4. confidante
    5. board
    6. squabbles
    7. appointee

III. Puting the sentences in the correct order:
    4. 6. 1. 5. 2. 7. 8. 3

IV. Vocabulary collocations.
    1. a-j
    2. e-h
    3. c-f
    4. b-i
    5. d-g

V. Matching the statements:
    1. d
    2. a
    3. c
    4. b
    5. e

Chapter 4: Two Orphans

I.True or false ? Justification:
1. False. They had the same parents because they were brothers.
2. False. The eldest boy was a pirogue man and the youngest one was a hunter.
3. False. He went there by his own initiative.
4. False.He was frightened.
5. False. The monster told the boy to cut off his hair.
6. False. He met the crocodile twice.
7. True. They were living in an undreground room in the case.
8. False. She told them to break down the eggs according to a predetermined order.
9. False. The youngest boy became a town chief, not the eldest one.
10. False. He died because he was burnt down by a heavenly fire.

II. Completing sentences:
1. aquatic
2. pirogue man
3. orphans
4. underground
5. trap
6. sacked
7. river

III. Putting sentences in the correct order:
3, 9, 7, 1, 8, 5, 4, 6, 10, 2

Chapter 5: The Ogre and the Boy

I. Comprehension answers.
1. They were afraid that their boy might be taken by the ogre.
2. They were agricultural workers.
3. The ogre ate some beans.
4. Glancing timidly at the ogre, the boy stayed motionless and tense.
5. The ogre came to the house twice.
6. No, they were very discontent.
7. The ogre was shot dead by the man and his corpse was thrown into a dump.

II. Writing questions:
1. Where did an ogre live?
2. Where did the man and his wife lock up their boy?
3. Where did the ogre and his wife go?
4. What did the ogre eat?
5. How did the ogre eat the beans?

III. Collocations matching the sentences:
1. d
2. c
3. b
4. a
5. e

IV. Matching the words in the box with their meanings.
1. recommendation
2. corpse
3. dump
4. to threaten
5. to glance at
6. beans
7. ogre
8. discontent

Chapter 6: A hunter'swoman and a Dog

I. True or false? Justification
1. False. They used to eat some fish and some meat
2. True. Whenever it was about to be bludgeoned by the hunter, the dog replied as a human being, by singing
3. False. She cheated her man three times
4. False. He went to hide in a bush near his house.
5. False. He rushed towards her and hit her with a stick

II. Matching the words with their meanings
1. h
2. c
3. b
4. g
5. d
6. e
7. f
8. a

III. Fill the gaps with the right verbs
1. eat/cook
2. roast
3. take
4. refrain
5. hide

IV. Completing the sentences
1. usually ate fish called « *Misangi* » ; ate neither cooked cassava nor other vegetables
2. the fish from the river
3. ate them and left nothing for her husband
4. got boiling mad but controlled his anger
5. claimed for his part of the fish

V. Completing the table
1. cooking/cook
2. hiding place/hideout
3. observation
4. food/feeding
5. hunter/hunting
6. realisation
7. gift
8. occurrence
9. reply
10. claimant

Chapter 7: A hunter, his Wife and their Dog

I. Choice of the right answer.
    1. c
    2. b
    3. b
    4. a
    5. c

*II. Match the statements in Table **A** with those in Table **B.***
    1. e
    2. c
    3. a
    4. b
    5. d

III. Completing the words from the tale.
    1. sign of protest
    2. gunpowder
    3. human being
    4. leaves of beans
    5. mushrooms

IV. Correcting these statements.
    1. The hunter and his wife had one dog.
    2. The hunter and his wife were living in a village called *Mulamba Lungandu.*
    3. The woman did not give the dog any food at meal time./ She gave the dog no food at meal time.
    4. The dog met its master near a large grove.
    5. The dog sang a protest song.

V. Putting the sentences in the correct order.
    6, 3, 1, 7, 9, 8, 2, 5

Chapter 8: The Robber of Bananas

I. Answers to the questions.
1. He planted pineapples, sugar canes, carrots, cassava, bananas, plantains and groundnuts.
2. Mamba hired some guards and kept a close watch on the field.
3. The robber dug up carrots, cassava and cut some sugar canes and pineapples. Afterwards he went to a river, drew near a banana tree to cut down a banana bunch.
4. The banana bunch started to sing.
5. The song reveals that Mamba has a father whose name is Makabu, that he usually eats groundnuts and wears rings on his navel.
6. The robber started to dance.
7. The robber slept under a banana tree.
8. No, the field owner caught the robber unobtrusively.

II. Making true sentences.
   Mamba: 4. 5. 7
   The robber: 1. 2. 3. 6. 8

III. Finding phrases in the tale.
   1. He had a large field.
   2. He had never been in a position to catch the robber.
   3. He came close to a banana tree.
   4. He was poised to cut down the banana bunch.
   5. He decided to hire some guards.
   6. Then he moved slowly and steallthily towards the robber.

Chapter 9: A Boy and a Man with a naked chest

I. Choice of the right answer.
   1. b
   2. c
   3. a
   4. b
   5. b
   6. c

II. Fill the gaps using words from the box.
   1. goats
   2. naked
   3. chest
   4. prostrate
   5. bride price
   6. presents
   7. bitterly
   8. adulthood

III. Putting the sentences in the right order.
   3, 4, 1, 5, 2, 10, 7, 9, 8, 6

Chapter 10: Two Boys and their Mothers

I. Answers to questions.
1. The two boys decided to build huts for their mothers.
2. The second boy mourned his mother very heavily.
3. The second boy descended his mother's corpse from the tree and put it into a game bag.
4. He had used veins cut from some palm trees.
5. He heard someone calling him.
6. The second boy threw his mother's corpse into a pond with stagnant waters.
7. A pretty girl got out of the pond with a brand new car.
8. They went to the girl's home.
9. She performed a magic gesture.
10. A lot of workers emerged/arrived to the court.

II. Finding phrases in the tale.
1. They were getting along well.
2. I don't want your mother to live with mine.
3. The boy climbed a tall tree.
4. The boy was observing him without saying anything.
5. The old woman said nothing.
6. The boy jumped up furiously towards her.

III. Finding the opposites.
1. old
2. near
3. girl
4. thin
5. short
6. to go away from
7. dry season
8. horrible
9. life
10. very old

IV. Fill the gaps using words from the tale.
1. cudgel
2. shelter
3. abundantly
4. rainy
5. pond
6. gamebag
7. furiously

V. Putting the sentences in the correct order.
9, 8, 7, 2, 1, 5, 3, 10, 4, 6

Chapter 11: A woman who killed her Son

I. Answers to questions
1. The woman regullarly went to the forest to haverst yams.
2. Her son asked to go with her to the forest to look for yams.
3. The woman cut yams into pieces, put them into a pan and cooked them.
4. The boy started to vomit and died.
5. The woman put her son's corpse onto an anthill and covered it with a small palm leaf.
6. The bird sang endlessly.

II. Matching the statements:
1. c
2. e
3. b
4. a
5. d

III. Fill in the gaps:
1. anthills
2. basket
3. son
4. puzzled
5. corpse
6. regularly/pan
7. palm

GENERAL GLOSSARY

amidst	among
appointee	someone who has been chosen officially for a position
bludgeon	a stout heavy club; club; it is thicker and loaded at one end
boar	a male pig
board	governing and organized body
bride price	the money or property brought by a bridegroom to his bride, dowry
chore	tedious, routine task, unpleasant job in a house
confidante	a trusted friend to whom secrets or private matters are disclosed
dazzled	stupefied by something overwhelming
discontent	dissatisfaction
dispirited	discouraged, in low spirits
dreadful	awful, terrible
emaciated	extremely thin
exhausted	very tired
feud	a bitter state of enmity
flatly	firmly and definitely
frightened	feeling fear
game bag	leather bag; it is used by hunters to carry killed animals

gleaming	shining
grove	a group of trees planted close together
harmlessness	innocence
hiding place	hideout, place where someone can keep hidden
household	domestic, in relation with the management of a house
indignant	slight indication
kaolin	a fine white clay
misdoer	someone who had carried out a bad action
mournfully	by weeping, shedding tears with grief and sorrow
naked:	wearing no clothes
navel	the small sunken mark on the surface of the abdomen
needle	a thin pointed bar used in knitting
odd	abnormal, bizarre
orphan	a child whose parents are dead
pebble	small roundish stone
pirogueman	someone who uses pirogues to transport people from one side of the river to the other side
pond	a still area of water; it is smaller than a lake
prediction	foretold event which will happen in the future
proposal	deal, offer

prostrate	reduced to extreme weakness
puzzled	filled with perplexity, at a loss
requirement	something which must be done
robber	someone who steals
rude	impolite
scales	Small hard flat pieces on the skin of a crocodile, a snake…..
shelter	refuge, protection, haven
skilled	sufficiently qualified, trained, experienced
sole	unique
sprawled	lying on the ground with arms and legs spread out
squabble	noisy quarrel
stealthily	without making any noise, with caution and secrecy
stump	a rooted remnant of a tree; the part of a tree which is left after most of the tree has been removed
tense	anxious and nervous
thorn	short hard pointed shrub of a plan tm of a plant
to barricade	to close off with a brocade ,a bulwark, a barrier
to be ensnared	to be cheated and caught out
to be filled with	to be full of

to be poised to	to be about to
to be twisted	to be bent into an abnormal shape
to break out	to start suddenly
to crisscross	to go all over, across
to curse	to utter maledictions
to dig up	to take out of the ground
to entrust someone with responsibilities	to give someone some specific tasks, duties
to feign	to make semblance of
to get along well	to be in good terms, to have good relationships
to get boiling mad	to be hopping mad, to become very furious
to lock up	to put someone, something into a safe place fastened by a lock
to resort to	to have recourse to
to stock up with	to keep supplies, to keep in store
to jeer at	to laugh derisively at
to knock out	to strike with a hard blow
to mourn	to weep with grief because of someone's death
to pave the way	to show the direction to a place
to pounce upon	to rush at, to jump on

to refrain from	to prevent from
to retort	to reply angrily and brutally
to run out	to come to an end, to diminish in quantity
to sack	to dismiss someone from a job, to deprive someone of an assignment
to scream	to cry loudly
to smash into	to hit very hard
to snigger	to laugh disrespectfully
to sob	to cry with an imploring voice
to stab	to pierce or to wound with a knife
to tackle a situation	to handle a situation, to deal with a situation
to take in	to swallow, to consume
to utter	to say, to emit audibly, to pronounce
trap	an object used for catching animals
uncouth	rough
unremitting	persistent
whimperer	someone who weeps with broken plaintive sounds
wrathful	full of anger
yam	a tropical plant. Its root is eaten as a vegetable

CURRICULUM VITAE OF THE AUTHOR

Christophe   KAMBAJI
Avenue du Derby, 7
Boîte 6
1050 Brussels
BELGIUM
Date of birth: 18 March 1944
Place of birth: Likasi (DRC)
Email : christophekambaji@outlook.com

EDUCATION
1971-Certificate in English Letters (University of Louvain)
1973Graduate in Germanic Philololgy (University of Brussels)
1977-Zerifikat Deutsch als Fremdsprache (Goethe Institut)
1979-Holder of the Agregation for teaching in High Schools and
  High Secondary Schools (University of Brussels)

PROFESSIONAL   EXPERIENCE
1973 - 1980-Teacher of English and German in High Belgian
  Secondary Schools and High Schools
1980 - 2004 -Teacher of English in High Belgian Secondary Schools
2004 - Retired teacher
2005 - 2010-English and French trainer in Belgian companies
2010- Teacher of Ciluba to adults (Université Libre   Internationale,
  Brussels)
2013- Teacher of Swahili to Belgian diplomats (The Language
  Center, Brussels)
2014 - 2017-Tutor in Belgian schools: English, French, Latin,
  Dutch, Mathematics

TRAININGS
2002 - Kent School of English (Broadstairs): The English
        Communicative Classroom
2012 - Cambridge University Press
2013 - Oxford University Press

The aim of these trainings : to help us improve our teaching methods

PROFILE
Communicative, team player, stress resistant, reliable eager to learn, organized, problem solving

PUBLICATIONS
1994 - Chinua Achebe: a *Novelist and a Portraitist of His Society*
        (Vantage Press, New York
2012 - *African Tales* (The Rose Dog Books, Pittsburgh, Ohio)

LANGUAGE SKILLS
Swahili: native speaker
French: fluent
English: fluent
German: fluent
Ciluba: fluent
Dutch: intermediate

INTERNET SKILLS
Word, WordPerfect, Excel, Internet

INTERESTS
I like reading novels, newspapers, magazines. I like classical music, African music
and in a selective way, world music

SPORTS AND HEALTH
Cycling, jogging and football.
Non -smoker